THE WAY HOME FOR WOLF

For Baby Sky, who made it here to us through the blanket of stars. We love you so much — R B

For Jodie, James, Rafe and Wilf — J F

ORCHARD BOOKS
First published in Great Britain in 2018
by The Watts Publishing Group
First published in paperback in 2019

1 3 5 7 9 10 8 6 4 2

Text © Rachel Bright, 2018
Illustrations © Jim Field, 2018

A CIP catalogue record for this book is available from the British Library

978 1 40834 921 2

Printed and bound in China

FSC
www.fsc.org

MIX
Paper from
responsible sources
FSC® C104740

Orchard Books, an imprint of Hachette Children's Group
Part of The Watts Publishing Group Limited
Carmelite House,
50 Victoria Embankment,
London EC4Y 0DZ
An Hachette UK Company
www.hachette.co.uk
www.hachettechildrens.co.uk

Rachel
BRIGHT

Jim
FIELD

THE WAY HOME FOR
WOLF

ORCHARD

As a rainbow of lights flickered soft in the night,
Dusting diamonds of ice in a desert of white,
The wild, whipping wind, it whistled its tune
To a howling of wolves and a shimmering moon.

And the loudest "ARrrroooOOO" in this echoing song
Was a wolfling called Wilf at the heart of the throng.
He loved to be fierce and longed to be grown.
He liked to try everything ALL ON HIS OWN.

"Look at me! I am big!
I am tough!" he would growl,

whilst he showed
off his strength

and practised his prowl.

One night it was time for the wolves to move on . . .

New folks had moved in and their shelter was gone!

So they left right away, to find a new cave.

They would have to walk far and they'd have to be brave.

"Let's go!" shouted Wilf, "I am ready to LEAD."

"You're too small," laughed the wolves, "it's an elder we need."

"One day," they advised, "you will guide from the front."

"I suppose," muttered Wilf with a huff and a grunt.

They struggled through snow as high as their flanks
And leapt over rocks as they scaled icy banks.

Wilf gave his all to keep pace and keep up,
But strong-willed as he was, he was still just a pup.

He kept dropping
back with each clamber
and climb,

as the pack journeyed
further away all the time.

Exhausted and breathless,
he strayed off the track

when a blizzard blew in . . .

. . . and he lost his way back.

Wilf longed to howl, "Help!"
and to holler it loud . . .
But his throat was too hoarse
and his heart was too proud.

He lay on the tundra,
his tail curled up tight.
A blanket of stars was
his bed for the night.
Until . . .

CRACK!
went the ice.
CRACK
and
KER-EEEEAK!

Wilf jumped to all fours
with a deafening shriek.

He stuck out the
claws on every limb.
He **HAD** to hold on . . .
because Wilflings can't swim!

Then he fell and he fell,
rolling and spinning.

It felt like the end,
but was just the beginning . . .

. . . since somebody down there had heeded his scream

And she swooped from beneath like a watery dream.

"I'll help you!" she called. "Just reach for my horn!"

A majestic and magical . . . SEA UNICORN!

Wilf's pride washed away and he stretched out a paw

As she lifted him gently back onto the shore.

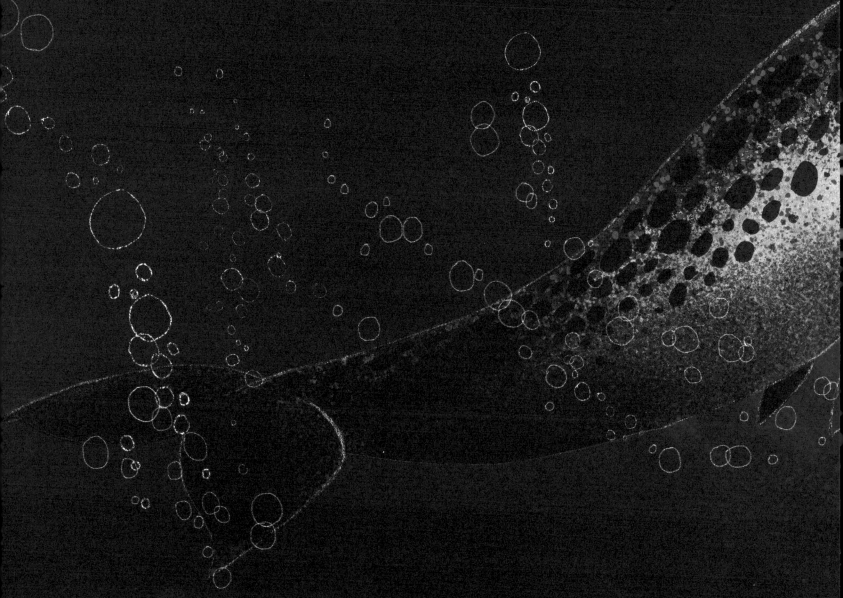

"Don't worry!" she sung
before dipping her brow,
"My friend **MR WALRUS**
will help you out now."

And there, right behind him, a huge, tusky fellow
Lifted his whiskers and let out a **BELLOW!**
"To the ridge!" he proclaimed with his chin in the air.
"My friend, mighty **MUSK-OX**, will take you from there."

And with waftings of fish and a very loud snort
Their journey was made and their travel seemed short.

And there, sure enough,
on the ridge was the ox,
Who took Wilf as far
as his friend . . .

... ARCTIC FOX

Who followed his nose
through the trees to a ...

... GOOSE

Who guided him,
honking, to ...

. . . this ancient **MOOSE!**

The moose knew these wilds
like no other soul.
He was steady and true
in pursuit of their goal.

And as twilight closed in,
Moose sang out a call
To a flittering, fluttering,
tiny fluffball . . .

A **BEAR-MOTH!** who showed
Wilf the rest of the way
To the place where this
wolfling most wanted to stay.

"THANK YOU!" Wilf waved
as he rejoined his pack,
And the wolves howled with joy
that their Wilfling was back.

They huddled him in and cuddled him close

And fussed over which wolf had missed him the most.

Wilf, he knew then, that when **ALL** come together

The darkest of times are easy to weather.

So he bowed to the narwhal, ox, walrus and goose,
And vowed to the fox, and the moth, and the moose . . .
"If ever I meet one who's strayed off their track,
I'll help them along by guiding them back."

And true to his word, Wilf is different now,

And his world seems much smaller and warmer somehow.

Since wherever life takes you, wherever you roam . . .

. . . we're all just a handful
of friendships from home.